DOG DAYS

BY DAVID LUBAR

AMELIA EARHART ELEMENTARY
OF INTERNATIONAL STUDIES
45-250 DUNE PALMS RD.
INDIO, CA

DARBY CREEK PUBLISHING

For Kelly Milner Halls,
who found this book a wonderful home

Published by Darby Creek Publishing,
a division of Oxford Resources, Inc.
7858 Industrial Parkway
Plain City, OH 43064
www.darbycreekpublishing.com

Text copyright © 2004 by David Lubar
Cover illustration © 2004 by Darby Creek Publishing
Cover illustration by Chris Sheban
Design by Keith Van Norman

Cataloging-in-Publication Data

Lubar, David.
Dog days / by David Lubar.
        p. cm.
ISBN 1-58196-013-1
Summary: Larry is enjoying the summer, playing baseball and taking care of the stray dogs he's brought home. Then his brother Paul finds another stray in an alley under mysterious circumstances, but the dog won't come home with them. When the price of dog food rises and the price paid for scrap falls, Larry has to find a new way to feed his dogs and try to help the dog from the alley.
1. Boys—Juvenile fiction. 2. Dogs—Juvenile fiction. 3. Brothers—Juvenile fiction. 4. Money—Juvenile fiction. [1. Boys—Fiction. 2. Dogs—Fiction. 3. Brothers—Fiction. 4. Money—Fiction.] I. Title.
PZ7.L96775 Do 2004
[Fic] dc22
OCLC: 52632266

Printed in the United States of America

First printing
2 4 6 8 10 9 7 5 3 1

CONTENTS

CHAPTER 1
A SPOT OF TROUBLE

Larry Haskins blocked the morning sun with his right hand and tried to spot the fly ball that was dropping from the sky. He caught sight of it high up, almost blending with a small patch of summer clouds.

"Got it!" Larry shouted. He brought his glove into position and dashed forward. There weren't many things as wonderful as the smack of a hard-ball landing dead center in the web of a well-oiled glove. It was especially wonderful because Adam Felcher had hit the ball. Last inning, Adam had caught Larry's line drive just before it would have sailed over the fence.

This was payback time—bottom of the ninth, two outs, the tying run on second.

Larry glanced away from the ball long enough to check the infield. The kid on second had reached third. Adam had rounded first and was tearing toward second. It didn't matter how far he got. He'd be out as soon as Larry made the play.

Plunging like a diving hawk, the ball was headed right for Larry's glove. Around the infield, his teammates yelled for him to make the catch. He tuned out the voices. Nothing existed in the world but the ball and his glove.

"Lar-r-r-ry!" A frightened shout ripped the air behind him. Startled, Larry glanced over his shoulder. His six-year-old brother, Paul, ran onto the field from a hole in the fence. "Larry, come with me! You have to come!" he yelled.

With a sudden rush of panic, Larry realized he'd taken his eyes off the ball. He flung his arm up. The ball hit the top of his glove and grazed off. It struck the ground, bounced against a rock, and skittered across the grass like a frightened rabbit.

Larry chased the ball. From the cheers that rose behind him, he knew that the tying run had already scored. He snatched the ball with his bare hand and spun, making the throw to Mark Tilly at second base just as Adam reached third. The throw was perfect. Mark caught it, turned toward the plate, and hurled a bullet to the catcher. Adam slid into home—just ahead of the throw.

"Safe!" the kid behind the plate called.

The whole time, Paul kept shouting, "Larry! Larry! Larry . . ."

Larry glared at his brother. "What are you doing in town?"

"Mom sent me to the store for a spool of thread," Paul said.

"Then go to the store," Larry said. "They don't sell thread here. They sell it *there*." He pointed past the field, down Washington Avenue, toward the row of little shops. "And stay on this side of the street."

"But, Larry, I think someone needs help." Paul grabbed Larry's wrist and started pulling. "Someone's in trouble. You've got to come."

"No," Larry said. "We're about to start another game." He was looking forward to getting back up to the plate. This time *nobody* would catch what he hit.

"It's important!" Paul stared up at Larry with eyes that seemed to say, *You're my big brother and you can fix anything.* Then he yanked at Larry's hand like he was trying to pluck an apple from a tree. "C'mon, pleeease!"

"All right, quit tugging." Larry couldn't refuse that pleading lost-puppy expression. And he realized there'd be no peace until he found out what Paul wanted. "I'll be right back," he called to his friends.

Carlos Montoya, who'd just arrived at the field, rushed in to fill Larry's spot. "Take your time, Larry. I've got it covered."

"This way," Paul said, climbing back through the hole in the outfield fence and trotting down Larch Street toward Washington Avenue.

Larry followed his brother, wondering what silly misunderstanding it would be this time. Last week, when they'd gone to the park with their parents, Paul yelled that he saw an alligator in the pond. The gator turned out to be a log. Sure, there was green moss on the log and rough bark that looked a little like a reptile's skin, but it was still nothing more than a wet log, which wasn't surprising since there wasn't a wild alligator within a thousand miles of where they lived.

Before that, there'd been burglars in the attic, a Martian in the backyard, a *Tyrannosaurus* in the woods, monsters in every possible hiding place throughout the house, goblins on the roof, and about fifty thousand other terrors—all springing from Paul's unstoppable imagination. He seemed to find something new to shout about every time he wandered away from where he was supposed to be.

As Larry followed his little brother along Washington Avenue, he wondered what could possibly happen on this quiet street in the middle of this quiet town. There wasn't any sign of a person in trouble—just a bunch of small stores and a couple of office buildings.

"Here . . . in the alley," Paul said when they'd gone halfway down the block. He dashed ahead, and then glanced back.

Larry caught up with his brother and looked into the alley that ran between the Reader's Roost Bookstore and LaGuardia's Diner, just half a block away from the shop where Paul was supposed to have gone. The narrow alley went from the sidewalk all the way to the back of the shops.

"What are you talking about? I don't see anyone," Larry said. Then he noticed something near the end of the alley—something that took him by surprise.

"Nice dog," Larry said. He stood a while, admiring the animal that was half-hidden in the shadows. The dog looked young, maybe a year or two old, about the size of a shepherd, but with a coat of short black hair. No collar or tags. *Could be part black Lab*, Larry thought. He knew every breed of dog on the planet. Besides baseball, there wasn't anything in the world he liked as much as dogs. Sometimes he thought he might even like dogs a little more than baseball. A ball had never wagged its tail when it saw him. A bat had never kept him company when he was sad.

Then Larry remembered why he'd let himself get dragged away from his baseball game. "I don't see anyone."

"No, not there," Paul pointed to the left side of the alley. "There! Look on the wall. Way in the back."

As Larry scanned the wall, his stomach tightened. A big red stain, five feet above the ground, was splattered against the side of the bookstore.

Still pointing to the spot, Paul said, "I think somebody got killed."

CHAPTER 2
THE MYSTERY MUTT

Larry stared for another moment, but quickly convinced himself that the spot on the wall couldn't be blood. "Relax, Paul. That's just paint or something. Come on. I'll show you."

"No," Paul said, shaking his head. He moved behind Larry.

"There's nothing to be afraid of," Larry told

him. He stepped into the alley, then froze as the dog bared its teeth, hunched down, and growled.

That's strange, Larry thought as he slowly backed away. *Dogs like me.* "Hi, boy," he said. "Nice dog."

The dog kept growling.

"I guess we're not getting any closer," Larry said. "But you can see from here—it's just paint." He searched the alley for evidence, an empty paint can or a brush or something. But nothing like that was in sight. The bookstore wall was blank except for the red splotch. The building didn't even have a window. A door at the side of the diner was closed. Three garbage cans stood next to the door. Two were round. The third one was the big, blue, square kind the town had started giving people for recycling.

Paul looked up at his brother and said, "It isn't paint. Paint would say something."

"Say something?" Larry asked.

"You know, like a name or a picture," Paul said.

"Oh, you mean graffiti. Okay, maybe it isn't paint. But even if someone got hurt, there's nobody around now who needs help. Come on, I'll walk you home." Larry wanted to go back to the game, but before that, he needed to check on his own dogs.

As Larry headed down the street, he kept glancing back. Even though the dog in the alley had growled, he halfway expected it to follow him. Dogs really did like him, no doubt about it. That was good, but it was also the cause of his biggest problem—just about every stray he met followed him home. The first time it happened, four years ago, he'd begged his parents to let him keep the dog. They'd said the dog could stay in the backyard until he found out where it belonged. Larry had cared for the dog for two weeks before the owner answered one of the "lost dog" posters he'd put up all over town.

Since then, Larry had helped out dozens of dogs. He almost always had at least one. He'd taken care of as many as four at a time. As hard as it was for him to give them away, he knew that each time he got a lost dog back where it belonged or found a new home for a stray, it meant he'd have room to help another dog.

Right now, he had three dogs in the backyard. His parents didn't mind, as long as he took good care of the dogs and bought all their food. His dad worked real hard every day, and his mom had a part-time job on the weekends, but there wasn't enough extra money to feed three dogs. Larry had already spent most of his savings on dog food. There was no way he could afford to feed another stray right now. Even if he had all the food in the world, the dog in the alley definitely didn't want to make friends with him.

When he was half a block away from his house, Larry could already see the dogs leaping and barking. They knew he was coming.

"Hi, boys," Larry said when he stepped through the gate in the backyard fence.

The dogs leaped all over him, licking his face, nipping at his shirt, and competing for his attention. "Good boys," Larry said. They were nice dogs that had somehow ended up on the street.

One of the strays—he'd named it Duke—was mostly shepherd. The others, Buck and Hobo, were mostly mixed, although Hobo was definitely part collie. Larry was careful about strays. His dad had a friend who worked for a vet, and the friend got each dog checked out. These dogs weren't sick or dangerous—just homeless. But Larry would make sure they were never homeless again.

"Want to help me feed them?" he asked Paul, who was still standing outside the fence.

"Yeah, but don't let them jump on me. Okay?"

"I'll try." Larry climbed the back porch steps and went into the kitchen. "I'm home," he said to his mom. "Paul's with me."

His mom sighed and shook her head.

"Thanks. I told him to come straight back."

As Larry lifted the dog food from the closet, he noticed how light the bag felt. *Time to buy another one*, he thought. Duke and Buck were adults, but Hobo was still growing, and he seemed to eat more each day.

The dogs went wild again when Larry brought the bag into the yard. "You can check the water," he told Paul as he filled the food bowls.

Paul dashed through the gate and grabbed the water bowl. He hurried over to the faucet at the back of the house while the dogs were busy chomping at the food.

"Thanks," Larry said when Paul set the bowl down.

Paul slowly reached out to pet Duke. But

when Duke lifted his head to sniff his fingers, Paul yanked his hand back.

"Go ahead," Larry said. "You know he won't hurt you."

Paul shook his head and stepped away from the dogs. "I think I'll go inside."

Larry had a hard time understanding how anyone could be afraid of the dogs. But he realized that to Paul, who had just finished kindergarten, the animals must seem pretty big.

Larry put the dog food away and went to his room. He took his bank down from the shelf next to his bed. He had twelve dollars—most of it from odd jobs he'd done around the neighborhood. He also collected aluminum cans and old newspapers and took them to the scrap yard every week. It was hard work, but there weren't many other ways a kid could earn money. Carlos, who had a paper route, was moving in September, and he'd promised Larry that he could take it over. Larry knew could make good money with a paper route. But fall was a long way off. For now, he'd just have to scrape by.

He took money from his bank, walked three blocks to the market, then went inside and headed down the pet-food aisle. As Larry reached out to grab the bag, he saw something that froze him where he stood.

"That can't be right," he said.

It had to be some kind of mistake.

CHAPTER 3

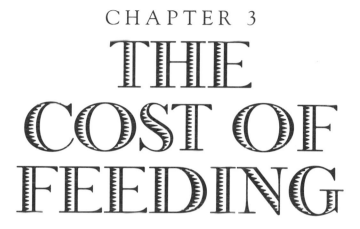

THE COST OF FEEDING

For a moment, Larry just stared at the sticker on the shelf below the bag of dog food. The price had gone up. And it hadn't gone up just a little. It had gone up a lot.

"Hey, mister," Larry said, spotting one of the market's managers at the end of the aisle. "I think there's a mistake on this price."

"Really? Let me see." The man pulled a small notebook from his pocket as he followed Larry back to the dog food. Then he bent down in front of the shelf.

"That's some big mistake," Larry said. "I'm sure glad I noticed it."

The man glanced at a page in his notebook, then back at the dog food. "No, it's right. They raised the price." He swept his hand past the different brands. "They all raised their prices. Sorry, kid. But that's the way it happens. Prices go up. Look on the bright side—your brand is still the cheapest." The man shrugged, then walked away.

Larry had no choice. The dogs needed the food no matter how much it cost. He bought the bag. Not only did he have to spend everything he'd taken from his bank, but he also had to go through his pockets to gather his change.

I'm not going to make it, he thought as he carried the bag down the street. The money that was left in his bank wouldn't even be enough for the next bag. He couldn't keep buying dog food unless he earned more money. Larry knew he couldn't ask his parents to help out. Some months they barely managed to pay all the bills and buy food for themselves. The walk home felt a lot longer than usual. And the bag on his shoulder felt heavier than ever before.

After Larry put the dog food in the closet, he sat down and tried to think of some ways to make more money. Later that afternoon, he'd go out to collect cans and newspapers, like he did every Monday. That was the best day of the week, because people wanted to get rid of the thick Sunday papers, and they seemed to drink more soda on the weekends. *I could ask the neighbors for work today*, he decided. He'd check at every house to see if there were any jobs he could do.

Usually whenever he asked around, somebody had some kind of chore for him. During the last year, Larry had painted a fence, washed nine cars, weeded several yards, trimmed a couple hedges, and cleaned out one attic, two garages, and a basement. He was tempted to start looking right away, but he remembered that most of the people in the neighborhood were at work. There was no point trying to talk to anyone yet.

Larry was in the mood to play more baseball. Paul and his mom had already eaten lunch, but she'd made a sandwich for Larry to take along. He grabbed his glove and headed back to the park. But as he walked and ate, Larry's mind wandered. Mostly, he thought about how he was going to earn money for the dog food. He also thought about the dog he'd seen in the alley. Larry was so lost in thought that he didn't pay any attention to where he was headed. When he looked up, he realized he was close to the diner. It was the tail end of the lunch hour and the place was busy, people coming and going like ants at a picnic.

I may as well take another look, he told himself. He sneaked up to the alley and peeked past the edge of the bookstore, wondering if the dog would growl at him again. In his mind, he saw himself making friends with it. He'd say calm words and get the dog to trust him.

But the dog didn't growl at him. It couldn't growl, because it wasn't there.

No reason for it to be here, Larry thought. Strays wandered. And there was no reason he should be looking for the dog. He absolutely couldn't take care of another stray, no matter how much it needed a home. But Larry was still bothered that it had growled at him. Dogs never did that.

A voice interrupted his thoughts. "Hey, are you going to play ball or just wander around town?"

Larry turned away from the alley. "Sure, I'm

going to play," he told Carlos. "I was on my way there."

"Then let's go."

Larry walked to the park with Carlos. They reached the ball field just as everyone was getting ready to choose up sides for a new game. Despite his worries, Larry managed to enjoy himself. The warmth of the sun on his face and the smell of his leather glove were a wonderful combination. He decided he wasn't going to let anything spoil his day.

This time when Adam hit a high fly, Larry caught it without any trouble.

On Larry's first turn at bat, he hit two fouls and took three balls. With a full count, he watched the pitcher. He knew that Steffi Shimoto almost always threw a high one over the middle on a full count. That was great, because Larry liked them a little high. Steffi went into her windup. The ball hurtled toward the plate, zooming in at just at the right height to be blasted over the fence.

Perfect, Larry thought, already seeing the home run in his mind. *You're going on a trip.* He stepped into his swing, eager to hear the solid crack that meant the ball was headed for orbit.

A frightened shout came from his left. "Larry! Lar-r-r-r-ry!"

CHAPTER 4

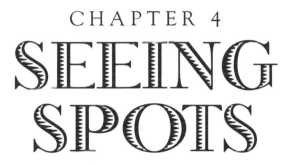

SEEING SPOTS

Larry was so startled that he forgot to swing. The only sound he heard came from the smack of the ball sinking into the catcher's mitt.

"Steeeeeeeeeerike three!" the kid behind the plate called. "You're out."

Larry dropped the bat and spun toward his brother. "Paul!" he yelled. "There is absolutely nothing I want to hear about right now—no monsters, no Martians, no dinosaurs, *nothing*. Do you understand?"

"It happened again," Paul told him. "There's more blood on the wall. I saw it. Honest. I wanted to get closer—" He stopped next to home plate, his chest rising and falling as he took deep breaths, looking up at Larry like his brother had the power to solve all the problems in the world. Paul caught his breath and continued, "But I couldn't. The mean dog was there again."

"The dog isn't there," Larry said.

"Is, too," Paul said.

Larry stepped away from the batter's box. "And you aren't supposed to be wandering around town."

"I wasn't wandering. Mom sent me back to the store because I forgot to get the thread."

34

"So, go get the thread." Even as he spoke, Larry imagined Paul wandering past the sewing shop and past the end of town and maybe not stopping until he reached the ocean.

"Please," Paul said, aiming those puppy eyes up at his brother.

"I give up."

Larry followed Paul to the alley. When they got there, he was surprised to find that Paul was right—the dog *was* back.

"See? I told you," Paul said.

Larry took a long look at the stray. The dog stared back. Larry felt it wasn't right for dogs to wander around town and hide in alleys. Every dog needed a home. Every dog needed someone to take care of it.

"See?" Paul said, pointing to the wall.

Larry's stomach tightened again when he noticed another spot on the wall. This one was lower than the first spot, and a couple of feet to the left. The dog growled when Larry tried to move closer.

"Easy there, boy," Larry said, backing away. He realized he'd missed a chance to examine the first spot earlier when the dog wasn't in the alley. Now there was another spot.

"What are we going to do?" Paul asked.

"We're going to stop worrying," Larry said. "Whoever put the paint there came back. That's all there is to it. It's just paint." But the more he listened to himself, the less he believed his own words.

"It isn't paint," Paul insisted.

Larry didn't feel like arguing. "Come on. Let's go."

"Are you playing more ball?" Paul asked.

Larry was about to say "yes," but he realized his brother wanted to hang out with him. "Would you like to do something?"

"Yeah!" Paul said, his face lighting up.

Larry grinned. He knew his brother enjoyed doing stuff with him. It would take Paul's mind off the spots in the alley. Larry realized it might even take his own mind off his problems.

"But let's get Mom's thread first," he said. "She's probably wondering why you aren't back yet."

After they finished the errand, they went to the pond and skipped stones. Then they went to the school and played on the seesaw. Larry had to sit real close to the center to balance Paul, but he enjoyed seeing his brother having fun.

"We'd better get home," Larry said after Paul had gone on the swings, the slide, and the jungle gym. "I have to collect cans and newspapers tonight."

"I'll help," Paul offered.

"Great. You can help me stomp on the cans to flatten them." Larry enjoyed having company when he hauled his wagon around the neighborhood.

After dinner, Larry headed out with Paul close behind.

"I'm looking for work if you've got anything that needs to be done," he told Mrs. Sherman when he reached his first stop.

"Sorry," she said, shaking her head. "I don't have any chores for you right now."

He went to the next house. And the next. At each house, Larry asked for work. At each house, the person at the door said one version or another of the same bad news: "Sorry. I don't need anything done right now. But I'll keep you in mind."

At each house, Larry said, "Thanks, anyhow," then collected the newspapers and cans and moved on. He didn't bother asking if anyone wanted a dog. He'd already asked his neighbors that question a dozen times before. This would *definitely* be the perfect time to find one of his three dogs a home. As much as he'd miss any of them, it would help the food last longer.

"Nothing, nowhere, no how," Larry said to

Paul as they left the last house. "Can you believe that? All these people, and nobody has a job for me."

"At least you have the cans and papers," Paul said.

"Yeah, at least I have those." Larry looked at the stack in his wagon. The papers were piled so high they were almost ready to topple. The cans, crushed flat, nearly filled a shopping bag. He headed for the small scrap yard that was just a couple of blocks from his house. The place closed at five, but the owner usually stayed late, and he always left the entrance unlocked on Mondays for Larry.

There was a chain wrapped around the gate, but no lock on the chain. "I can always count on Mr. Penwood," Larry told Paul. He unwrapped the chain, swung the gate aside, and pulled the wagon carefully through the opening. That's when he saw the sign.

"Oh, no!" Larry groaned.

Just when he was sure that things couldn't get any worse, Larry found out that they could. They sure could.

CHAPTER 5

SCRAP THAT PLAN

"What's wrong?" Paul asked.

"That," Larry said. He pointed to the piece of cardboard taped to the fence beside the gate.

Paul stared at the sign. "I can't read. What does it say?"

"It's the price he's paying for paper and aluminum," Larry told him. "It went down. I won't get as much as I thought."

"Maybe it's a mistake," Paul said.

"No such luck," Larry answered, shaking his head. He'd learned that lesson at the market—prices changed. But why did they always have to change in the worst possible way? Why couldn't the price of dog food go *down* and the price of scrap metal go *up*? He guessed it was for the same reason that dogs wandered the streets and people got sick—life wasn't always fair.

"Well, it's not good, but it's better than nothing," Larry said, sighing. He pulled his wagon along the gravel path that led to the scales.

Fang, the dog who guarded the scrap yard, snarled and rushed out from the shed where he lived. But as soon as he recognized Larry, he wagged his tail. Two years ago, Larry had found the dog huddled and shivering in the rain by the bowling alley. It was barely more than a puppy back then. He'd brought it home, cared for it, and named it Lucky. Mr. Penwood, who owned the scrap yard, wanted a dog. He'd given Lucky a new home and a new name. "Scrap yard dogs need tough names," he'd explained. "Now he's Fang."

Paul moved behind the wagon, putting it between himself and Fang.

"Hi, boy," Larry said, petting the dog. "Mister Penwood, I'm here at the scale," he shouted.

"Be right with you," a voice called from the other side of a pile of tires. "Go ahead and load it up."

Larry stacked the newspapers on the scale.

"Let's see what you have," Mr. Penwood said

as he walked up to the scale. He slid the weights at the top, squinted at the numbers, then took the papers off the scale and weighed the cans.

"Okay, eight plus seven is fifteen, carry the one . . ." He mumbled a bit more, scrunched his brows as if thinking, then dug into his pocket and pulled out a handful of coins. "Sorry about this," he said as he counted out the money, "but there's so much scrap that the prices had to go down. Everybody's recycling. Especially now with the new town law. Supply and demand. That's life, I guess."

"Thanks." Larry took the money. *This isn't going to help very much*, he thought. He knew he had to find some way to earn more. There wasn't anything else he could do that evening.

But tomorrow he'd search all over town. Surely someone would have some kind of work for a kid. He was willing to do anything—the dogs couldn't go without food. If he wasn't able to feed them, he'd have to take them to the dog pound. He didn't even want to think about that.

"Here, this is for helping." Larry gave his brother a dime.

"Wow, thanks," Paul said. He looked down at the coin in his palm as if he'd been handed a sack of gold. "Dad said a penny saved is a penny earned. So I guess this is ten pennies earned. Right?"

"Right." That gave Larry an idea. He hated to ask, but he didn't have much choice. "Hey, Paul, do you have any money saved up?"

"Yeah. I have a whole bunch," Paul said.

"Really?" Larry's heart beat faster at the news. "How much?"

"Three dimes and two quarters," Paul said. "Four dimes now," he added, grinning. "That's a lot, isn't it? I'm almost rich."

"Yup, that's a lot." Larry realized that Paul's life savings weren't going to be any help. He gave Fang another pat on the head. The dog rolled over and let Larry rub his belly.

"Come on," Larry said to Paul. "He wants you to scratch him."

Paul inched over, taking small, shuffling steps like someone crossing an icy sidewalk. He reached out and gave Fang's belly a quick scratch, then jerked his hand away.

Larry waited until it was obvious that Paul

wasn't going to try again. "Let's go," he said. "Come on, I'll give you a ride."

Larry pulled the wagon home. When he got there, he went into the yard to feed the dogs again.

"Hey, guys, have you ever thought about going on a diet?" he asked as he watched Buck, Hobo, and Duke gobble up the food. They didn't answer him with words. Instead, they filled the air with crunching sounds. In the bowls, the chunks of dry food disappeared like coins in a magician's hand.

After the dogs finished attacking the food, they attacked Larry with paws and tongues and wet noses. He fell on the ground and rolled around with them, buried in an avalanche of furry affection.

It's worth it, he thought as he scratched Buck behind the ear with one hand and pushed Duke's muzzle away from his own ear with the other. Whatever he had to do to keep these dogs fed, it was worth it. He petted Buck, remembering how scared and nervous the dog had been when Larry first found him. Somebody had mistreated Buck. Hobo, on the other hand, had always been a clown. And Duke, who had lots of energy, was the leader of the pack.

As Larry played with the dogs, he found himself thinking about the dog in the alley. Why did it growl? Where did it eat? Did anyone ever pet it? He knew that if he brought the dog home, it would stop growling at him. Maybe it would even become as friendly as these three.

"Don't even think about doing that," he said out loud.

Hobo cocked his head and stared at Larry when he spoke. Larry laughed and petted the dog. "Don't worry. I'm just talking to myself. I found a new friend for you, but I get the feeling you'll never meet him."

Larry got up and went inside, carrying the nearly empty bag with him. He'd have to open the new bag soon. And once it was opened, it wouldn't last long. *I'll come up with some way to make money tomorrow*, he thought as closed the back door. *I have to.*

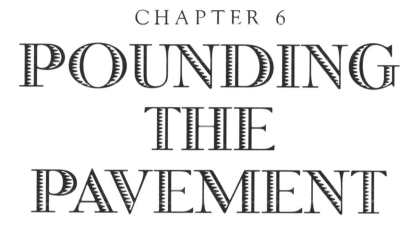

CHAPTER 6
POUNDING THE PAVEMENT

The next morning Larry got up early, which was nice because it gave him a chance to have breakfast with his dad. After his dad left for work, Larry walked over to the kitchen window. A hot breeze lifted the curtains and blew against his face. It was going to be a perfect day for baseball. In an hour, everyone he knew would be out at the field, pitching and hitting and running and sliding. But no matter how much he wanted to play ball, Larry wouldn't be there.

He headed toward a different part of town. The east side was closer, but there were more stores on the west side, so Larry decided to go there first. With all the shops that lined the streets, he figured someone would have work for him. He didn't care what the job was—just as long as he made enough money to feed his dogs.

He tried the barbershop. "Need someone to sweep up?" he asked. "I'm a hard worker."

"No, thank you," the barber said, pointing to the row of empty chairs. "Business is a little slow right now."

He tried the pet shop. "Need someone to

clean the cages? I'm really good with animals. Especially dogs."

"I already have someone doing that," the owner said. "Sorry."

Larry tried the hardware store, the music store, two supermarkets, and three restaurants. No one had any work for him. He tried the movie theater, the hat shop, and both pizza places. Still no luck. He even tried a store that sold wedding gowns and another place where he wasn't sure *what* the people did.

By early afternoon Larry had tried nearly all of the shops on the west side of town. Not a single person had a job for him. He needed a break. He'd heard so many people say "no" that he felt he deserved a little fun. Larry decided to get his glove and play some ball. His stomach kept reminding him that it was past lunchtime, so he planned to grab a sandwich, too.

Larry cut over to the east side and walked past the alley on his way home. Sure enough, the dog was there again. And sure enough, it growled when he tried to get close.

"Nice doggie," Larry said, using his most soothing voice. "Good dog. You're a nice dog, aren't you?" Most dogs came running when he talked like that.

Not this dog. It just kept growling.

"Someday," Larry said, "you're going to stop growling at me. You'll see."

Larry went home. "Nice doggie," he said to Hobo when he reached the back yard. "Good dog."

Hobo licked Larry's face. So did Buck and Duke.

"Now *that's* how a dog's supposed to act," Larry said. He noticed that Paul was watching him from the kitchen window. Larry motioned for his brother to come out, but Paul shook his head.

I wish Paul would stop being afraid, Larry thought as he went inside.

"We waited for you," his mom said. "Ready for lunch?"

"Sure."

"Me, too," Paul said. "I was just about starving. I thought you'd never get home."

His mom made sandwiches—peanut butter for Paul, chicken salad for herself, and turkey for him. After he ate, Larry grabbed his glove.

"Want to come to the field?" he asked Paul.

"I thought you didn't like it when I came," Paul said.

Larry shook his head. "I don't mind. And at least this way, I won't have to worry about you surprising me in the middle of my swing."

Only a couple of kids were at the field when Larry and Paul got there. Paul ran over to the tire swing that hung from a tree behind the backstop. Larry tossed the ball around with the other kids and waited for enough players to show up for a game.

When Mark and Adam arrived, Larry asked them, "Which way did you guys come?"

"The usual," Mark said. "Down Washington to Larch. Why?"

"I was wondering if you saw a dog in the alley by the bookstore."

"Nope," Adam said. "Didn't notice one."

"Are you looking for another dog?" Mark asked.

"No way. That's the last thing I need." Larry wondered about the dog again. It had been there earlier, but now it was gone. *It's just like keeping track of Paul,* he thought. Except Paul rarely growled at him.

"Hey, Larry," Carlos said as he walked onto the field.

"Hi," Larry said, tossing the ball to his friend. Carlos's voice sounded funny. "Is something wrong?" Larry asked.

Carlos tossed the ball back, but he didn't look

at Larry. "It's just . . ." He shook his head and stared across the field at the road.

"Come on," Larry said. "What is it?"

"Listen," Carlos said, "I hate to tell you this, but I've got some bad news."

CHAPTER 7

AS BAD AS IT GETS

"Bad news?" Larry asked Carlos. "What about?"

"You know how I promised you could have my paper route when I moved away this fall?" Carlos asked.

"Sure," Larry said. "I've been counting on it."

"Well, things have kind of changed," Carlos said, kicking at a rock in the dirt.

"You aren't moving?" Larry guessed. "Is that

it? Your folks decided to stay in town? Hey, that's not so bad. At least you'll still be around. So that's really good news." Larry understood what people meant when they said they had "mixed feelings." He hated the thought of not getting the paper route, but he was glad his friend wasn't going away.

Carlos shook his head. "I wish that was it. I'm still moving. But my cousin is coming to town. My mom's making me give him the paper route. I told her I promised to give it to you, but she says family comes first."

"Oh, man . . ." Larry didn't know what else to say. Everything was supposed to get better in the fall. That's all that had kept him going. Now it looked like things would never get better. He felt like he'd just opened a huge bag of dog food and found that it was filled with nothing but hard clumps of dirt.

"Hey, I'm sorry," Carlos said. "I really wish I could give it to you."

"Yeah, I know. It's not your fault," Larry said.

"So," Carlos asked, "are we going to play some ball?"

"Not right now," Larry said. "Maybe later." He went over to get Paul.

"We're leaving?" Paul asked.

Larry nodded. He walked off the field with Paul and headed toward home. No matter how much he loved baseball, he just couldn't enjoy the game right now. He needed to be with his dogs.

They were waiting for him. Paul went inside. Larry stayed in the yard. He played with the dogs and brushed them. "I don't know what I'm going to do, guys. But don't worry," he told them. "I'll figure out something. I'm not going to let you down."

Shaking his head, Larry filled the water bowl for the dogs and got them some food. He finished the last of the old bag and opened the new bag. He looked from the full bag to the crumpled, empty sack. It was amazing how quickly one turned into the other. Unless he got some money real soon, there was no way he'd be able to keep feeding the dogs.

Larry spent the rest of the afternoon playing with the dogs and trying to think of a way to make money. *Maybe I can sell some of my stuff*, he thought. He realized he had hardly anything worth selling. He looked at the porch where he'd left his glove. The glove was only a year old—just now perfectly broken in. He could get some money for it, but he didn't know if he could bear to give it up.

Larry scratched Duke behind his left ear and rubbed Hobo's back. "I'll sell my glove if I have to, guys. That's a promise. Like Carlos said, family comes first. And you're part of the family."

"Larry, it's almost six," Paul called from the back porch. "Mom says to come in for dinner."

As Larry walked into the house, he thought about the strange things he'd seen during the past two days. He thought about the dog in the alley and he thought about his own life. As much as every day seemed different, he realized that most things fell into cycles and patterns. Dinner at six. Baseball in summer. School in September.

Every week his parents paid bills. Every week he collected papers and cans. Every weekday his dad went to work. Every weekend his mom went to her job. Patterns and cycles, cycles and patterns. Over and over.

He knew there were things he could always count on. He could always count on Paul to wander. He could always count on kids showing up at the park to play ball. And just like his dogs could count on him, he could always count on his parents to make meals. Breakfast, lunch, and dinnertime, someone was always there for him. But who was there for the dog in the alley?

"Dinnertime!" he said out loud.

Everything fell together in Larry's mind. There *was* an answer. Larry knew what he needed to do tomorrow. He was so excited, he had a hard time falling asleep that night, but finally, he drifted off.

When Larry awoke the next morning, it was too early to try his plan. So he got dressed, fed his dogs, and played with them for a while. Finally, late in the morning, he searched for Paul. He found him watching cartoons in the living room.

"Come on," Larry said. "I've got something to show you."

"Where are we going?" Paul asked.

"You'll see," Larry said, feeling a little like one of those detectives in the movies. "I have a plan."

I sure hope I'm right, he thought.

Larry knew this could be his last chance to

save his dogs. It was the bottom of the ninth, bases were loaded, and he was down to his last swing.

CHAPTER 8

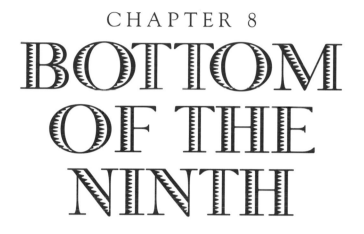

BOTTOM OF THE NINTH

Larry and Paul headed into town. As they reached the alley, the dog came up from behind them and darted past, heading between the bookstore and the diner.

I knew it! Larry thought. He looked across the street at the clock in front of the bank. Then he looked through the big glass windows of the diner. There was almost nobody inside. "Any minute now," he said.

"What do you mean?" Paul asked.

"Just wait." Larry was sure it would happen soon—if he was right. He watched the dog in the alley. It sat facing the door on the side of the diner.

Five minutes passed. The dog sat still. Only its ears moved with every tiny noise.

"Nothing's happening," Paul said.

"Be patient," Larry told him.

Five more minutes passed. Larry started to wonder if he was wrong.

Suddenly, the dog got an excited look—the same look Larry saw on his dogs' faces every time he dragged out their bag of food.

"Watch," he whispered to Paul

An instant later, the side door opened. A man wearing a white apron stuck his head out from inside the diner. "Here, pooch! Nice pooch," he called into the alley. The dog barked and wagged its tail. The man held out a plate and flipped something off it. The stuff bounced off the opposite wall, left a splotch, and landed on the ground. The dog gobbled it up.

"Leftovers," Larry explained. "After breakfast, lunch, and dinner, when the rush is over, that guy throws some food to the dog. That explains why it was only here at certain times. It must be pretty smart to have figured that out. That also explains why it growled—to protect the place where the food came from. The spots are just ketchup and stuff like that."

Larry turned away from the alley and walked

toward the front door of the diner. Now that he knew he was right, he hoped the second half of his plan would go smoothly. Especially since this was the part that would save *his* dogs.

"Where are we going?" Paul asked as he followed Larry.

"To talk to someone." Larry went inside the diner. The place was almost empty, but Larry was sure it had been crowded an hour earlier when the people were eating breakfast.

"Take a seat anywhere," the waitress said. "I'll be right with you."

"Is the owner here?" Larry asked.

The waitress nodded and went through a door behind the counter. A minute later, the man in the white apron came out. "What's up, boys?" he asked. "Got a complaint?"

"No. No complaint. I saw you feeding that dog," Larry said. "I wanted to tell you that's a real nice thing to do."

The owner shrugged. "It would just get thrown out otherwise," he said.

"Are you careful what you give him?" Larry asked. "Some scraps aren't good for dogs."

"What are you, some kind of dog expert?" the owner asked. "Of course, I'm careful. I like animals."

"Good. I'd hate to see him eating the wrong things. I've got three dogs myself. They sure do eat a lot. It's tough feeding them. But if you're just throwing out the leftovers, you wouldn't mind if I took some, right?" Larry held his breath, waiting to see if the man would accept his offer.

The man looked at Larry for a moment, as if trying to make a decision. "I'll tell you what," he finally said. "I'm supposed to sort everything for recycling—you know, paper, metal, plastic. It's a new law in town. But I'm so busy that it's hard to find the time. If I don't do it right, I'll have to pay a big fine. I could use some help. You willing to work hard?"

"Absolutely," Larry said.

The man reached under the counter and pulled out a pair of rubber gloves. "If you sort the recyclables for me, you can take anything that your dogs can eat. It wouldn't just be scraps. Sometimes there's an extra roast at the end of the day. We don't keep stuff overnight." He pointed to a sign that read, "ALL OUR FOOD IS MADE FRESH EVERY DAY."

"If you do a real good job, I'll even see if I can pay you a couple of bucks each week. What do you say?"

"That's great!" Larry said. It was more than great. With the food from the diner, he'd be able to stretch out the bags of dog food. There'd be enough for all of the dogs. Larry couldn't believe his luck.

"I just have one condition," the owner said.

Here it comes, Larry thought. He knew there had to be a catch. Just like with the price of food. And the price of scrap. And now, the price of food scraps. "What's the condition?" Larry asked.

The owner pointed toward the side door. "That nice pooch out there. He needs a home, too. Can you take care of him?"

"Sure," Larry said before he had time to think. But even after he thought about it, he knew it was exactly what he wanted to do. "You've got a deal." He shook hands with the owner. Then Larry turned to Paul. "Come on. You can help me sort the recyclables."

While he worked, he tossed a bit more food out to the dog, both to keep it from straying and to get it used to him. A half hour later, Larry left the diner with a large, stuffed bag of food. He and Paul walked out the door that led to the alley.

The dog backed away a step, but it didn't growl.

"Here, boy," Larry said.

The dog cautiously walked over to him and sniffed the bag. Then it walked past him and started sniffing Paul.

Paul backed away a step, but didn't call for help. The dog followed him. Paul backed off another step. The dog followed him again. Larry watched carefully to make sure Paul was safe, but he didn't get between them.

"Nice doggie," Paul said. He reached out, then hesitated and looked up at his brother.

Larry nodded. "Go on. Real slow. Real gentle."

Paul put his hand on the dog's back and petted him. "Nice doggie," he said again.

"He *is* nice," Larry agreed.

Paul scratched the dog's head, and the dog licked his hand. "What are you going to call him?" Paul asked.

"What else?" Larry said, looking across the

alley at the wall. The perfect name was right in front of his eyes. "We're going to call him Spot."

"I like it," Paul said.

"Thanks for bringing us together," Larry said. He realized that he might never have met the dog if his brother didn't have such a wild imagination. And he realized something else. "You know what? This isn't just my dog, Paul. It's *our* dog. Yours and mine."

Paul looked up at Larry and grinned. "He likes me." Then he went back to petting Spot.

Larry grinned, too. He walked toward the street with the two wanderers tagging along behind him.

"Come on, Spot," he called. "We're going home."